For Esme and Henry and for Jess, my super supportive mum – S.C.
For Max and Matthew – G.M.

First published in 2020 by Nosy Crow Ltd

The Crow's Nest, 14 Baden Place

Crosby Row, London, SE1 1YW

www.nosycrow.com

ISBN 978 1 78800 768 9 (HB) • ISBN 978 1 78800 769 6 (PB)

Nosy Crow and associated logos are trademarks

and/or registered trademarks of Nosy Crow Ltd.

Text copyright © Stephanie Clarkson 2020 • Illustrations copyright © Gwen Millward 2020

The right of Stephanie Clarkson to be identified as the author and of

Gwen Millward to be identified as the illustrator of this work has been asserted.

A CIP catalogue record for this book is available from the British Library.

Printed in China

Papers used by Nosy Crow are made from wood grown in sustainable forests.

1 2 3 4 5 6 7 8 9 10 (HB)

1 2 3 4 5 6 7 8 9 10 (PB)

Super Milly
and the
Super School Day

STEPHANIE CLARKSON

GWEN MILLWARD

 nosy crow

I am SUPER MILLY!

Today is **Superhero Day** at school.

I have used all the tinfoil,
a tea towel with only one hole
– which doesn't even show –
a pair of my brother Joe's pants,
and a **big badge** with an **M**.

But . . .

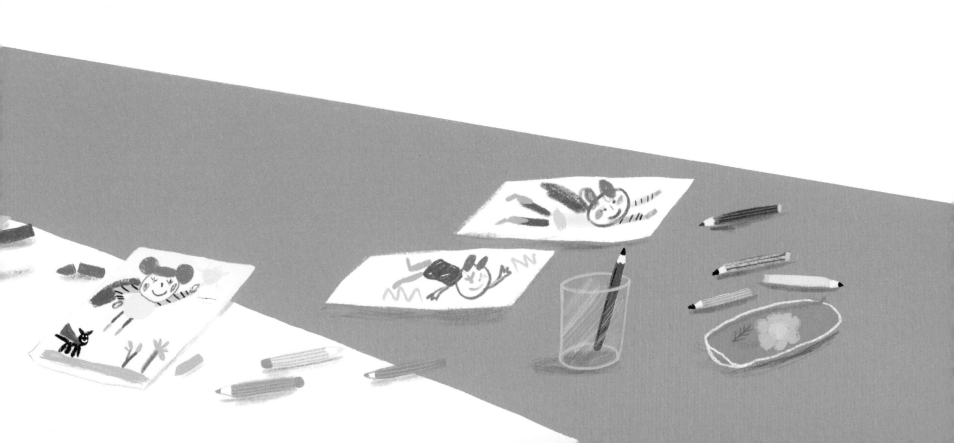

. . . I don't have
X-ray vision . . .

I can't **climb
up buildings . . .**

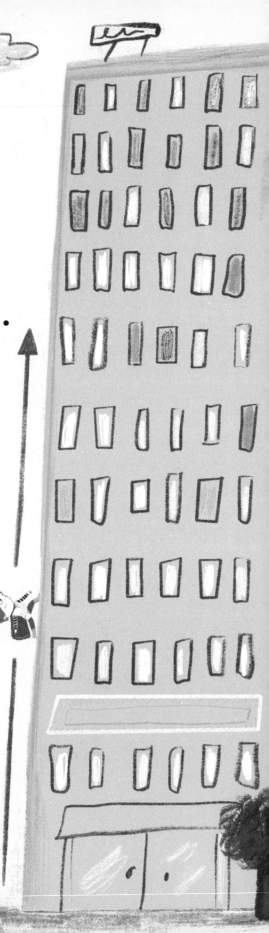

and **superheroes** are supposed to
beat the baddies . . .

but I can't stop Joe taking
the last bit of toast.

I don't have **any** special powers.

When I get into class, there is already a big **emergency**.

William's dad has forgotten that it is Superhero Day. William is crying in the book corner . . . in his normal trousers!

A **real superhero**
would spin around
William **super fast . . .**

until his outfit changed.

But Miss Kent says, "Bottoms
on seats please, Milly."

So, I think hard and . . .

. . . I unpin my special badge.

"You can be **Wonder William**," I say.
"But it's an **M**," he says.
I pin it on him upside down.
"Now it's a **W**!"

BAM!

Wonder William says
I am **super** kind.

Next, we have to write about
"A Day in the Life of a **Superhero**".

Fantastic Flora is not keen on writing.

Her **b**s keep looking like **d**s.

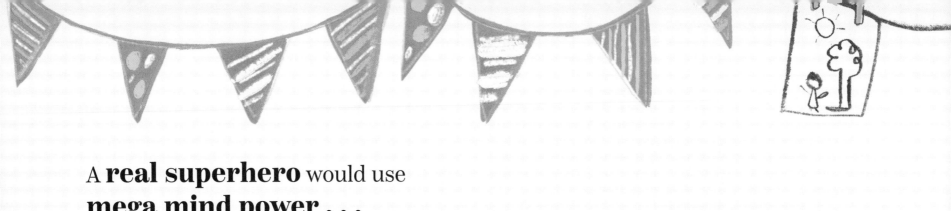

A **real superhero** would use **mega mind power . . .**

to make Flora's pencil write all by itself!

But the pencil stays still. William says it moved, but that's because he pushed it a bit with his finger.

I think really hard and . . .

. . . "Hey, Flora!" I say. "What has a cape and goes round and round?

A superhero in a washing machine."

KABOOM!

Fantastic Flora says I am **super** funny and writes down the joke all by herself.

In the afternoon, we do art.

Amazing Archie wants to paint a supervillain,
but **Spider Sid** is hogging the green paint.

A **real superhero**
would grab the green . . .

and fly at **super speed**
between Archie and Sid,
so that they can share.

But my flying cape
is trapped under
my apron!

I think really,
really hard and . . .

... "We can mix blue and yellow together to make green!" I say.

ZAP!

Amazing Archie is amazed and says I am **super** clever!

He loves green so much he paints **everything** – including William!

It is nearly home time.

Incredible Iqbal has brought in a minibeast for Show and Tell. Spider Sid says it is really rubbish and not even a tarantula. Iqbal's voice goes all quiet . . .

and then the spider escapes!

There is a **lot** of screaming . . .

. . . until Fantastic Flora
catches it again.

But Spider Sid is laughing
and pointing at me and Iqbal.

A **real superhero** would
make a **force field** around us,
so no one can hurt our feelings.

But it's hard to do force fields when you are turning as red as a tomato.

I do some supersonic thinking and . . .

. . . have a brilliant idea!
I hold hands with Iqbal, and our
superness gets stronger . . .

Then, in my **loudest** voice, I tell the class
that spiders have blue blood and can spin
silk. Iqbal's voice comes back, and he spells
out the name for the fear of spiders –

"ARACHNOPHOBIA."

WHIZZ!

Incredible Iqbal says
I am **super** brave.

WHAM!

Everyone claps and says
I am a **super** good friend.

Spider Sid does a
really loud cheer.

I am **SUPER MILLY!**

Maybe I **do** have special powers after all . . .

BAM!

I am kind.

KABOOM!

I am funny.

ZAP!

I am clever.

WHIZZ!
I am brave.

WHAM!
I am a good friend.

These are **my** superpowers!

KERPOW!
I bet **you** have superpowers too.